This Book Belongs
MW00890544
01

DESTINY IMAGE® PUBLISHERS, INC.
P.O. Box 310, Shippensburg, PA 17257-0310
"Promoting Inspired Lives."

This book and all other Destiny Image and Destiny Image Fiction books are available at Christian bookstores and distributors worldwide.

For more information on foreign distributors, call 717-532-3040.

Or reach us on the Internet: www.destinyimage.com

ISBN 13 HC: 978-0-7684-5695-0
ISBN 13 EBook: 978-0-7684-5696-7
ISBN 13 TP: 978-0-7684-5806-0

For Worldwide Distribution, Printed in the U.S.A.

1 2 3 4 5 6 7 8 9 10 11 / 27 26 25 24 23 22 21 20

GREAT ADVENTURES PRODUCTIONS
A One Voice Ministries Publication
Hankandbrenda.org
PO Box 390460
Omaha, NE 68139

One hot morning in July, Mutzphey and Milo were playing baseball.

It was Mutzphey's turn to bat. "Come on! Give me your best pitch! I'll hit it to the moon!" he cried, as he swung at the pitch...and missed.

"Strike three! Yerrrr out!" yelled the umpire. "They win!"

Mutzphey was determined to show everyone that he could have hit a home run if he'd wanted, so he ran around the bases as fast as he could.

Exhausted, he fell across home plate.

"Come on, Milo.
I let them win anyway. They were
being too computertive."

"Ha! You mean 'competitive,'"
said Milo.

"Yeah, yeah, whatever.
Let's go to my house
and get some cold lemonade,"
said Mutzphey.

As Mutzphey guzzled his drink, he suddenly had a bright idea.
"We should open a lemonade stand and sell ice-cold drinks across the USA... and the whole wide world!"
"Milo, I'll bet we'd make a million dollars in one day if we sold each cup for a dime!"
M

"We'll get rich, rich, really rich!
Can you see it, Milo? Money, money,
money, lots of green money..."

"Mutzphey, snap
out of it!" yelled Milo.
"We shouldn't be greedy."

"Sure, sure, sure," said Mutzphey, "but imagine what we could buy with a million dollars."

So, off they went to build their lemonade stand.

Mutzphey listed all of the things he would get, once they got some serious cash.

"I'm getting a faster bike, Galaxy Game System 7, tons of new video games, every issue of Captain Zepto comics, that fancy fishing rod I've been wanting, all of the Space Heroes action figures..."

This list went on and on and on...and...on.

As they sat all day at their new stand, the sun grew hotter and hotter.

Meanwhile, not one customer came by.

"Hey, Milo, how much money do we have now?" asked Mutzphey.
"Not one cent since YOU drank all the lemonade," muttered Milo.

Together, they decided to make a bigger sign and a fresh batch of lemonade. Surely they'd get some customers now!

Still, no one bought their lemonade.

"I'm sooo thirsty, hungry, frail, and weak. I've got to have something to drink!" wailed Mutzphey, grabbing a cup of lemonade and putting on quite a show.

"YUCK!"

yelled Mutzphey, gagging. "I'm going to throw up! This is the worst lemonade I've ever tasted!"

OOPS! Milo had mistaken the salt for sugar when making the lemonade.

Mutzphey yelled, “Now I know why people are staying away by the thousands – it’s because you can’t cook, Milo!”

"Yeah? Well, if you weren't so loud and obnoxious, maybe people would come," said Milo, sticking out his tongue.

"Who are you calling ob-NOT-shucks?!" asked Mutzphey. "You're just a big baby."

"You know what Mutzphey? That's it! Sticks and stones will break my bones and the names you call me hurt me."

"I QUIT!" Milo shouted, as he turned to leave.

As he did, Mutzphey grabbed him. "Ack! Let me go!" Milo yelled.

"No way!" answered Mutzphey.

The two scrapped and scuffled until Milo managed to squirm away.

The next day things got worse for the two arguing friends. They opened separate stands across the street from each other.

Mutzphey shouted "If you like salty lemonade, Milo's got gallons!"

The sour competition escalated minute by minute as the two frantically lowered their prices, made bigger signs, and tried flashier gimmicks.

Milo loudly rapped from his stand,

"Listen up!
If you like bad lemonade,
Mutzphey's got it made! -
So stick with mine,
It's fresh all da TIME!"

After a long day, they both went home, as divided as they had ever been.

As Milo knelt to say his prayers, a Bible verse dropped into his heart:

"Forgive one another as the Lord has forgiven you."

Milo began to pray, "God please help me to forgive Mutzphey because he's acting mean."

Suddenly, Milo realized that he had been just as mean as Mutzphey.

"I've got to apologize," he said, calling as fast as he could.

Mutzphey answered, "I'm sleeping!!" and hung up.

The next morning, Milo sat at his stand completely unaware of Mutzphey's latest plan when...

...a water balloon hit him right in the kisser!

"Is that all you got?" asked Milo, trying to act tough.

"Incoming water missile!" yelled Mutzphey, grabbing a garden hose and squirting Milo.

Cold water ran down Milo's beak, all the way to his toes. He was completely soaked. He headed home.

"That's right! Go and tattle to your mommy!" mocked Mutzphey.

At Milo's house, his parents reminded him that God wants us to forgive others and be kind.

Just then, they heard a very loud noise. It was Mutzphey hollering, "Chocolate lemonade! Get your chocolate lemonade!"

But still, no one came to his stand.

Day after day, Mutzphey's situation grew worse and worse, while Milo's business got better and better.

Everyone from all over the neighborhood came to get some of Milo's lemonade. He started selling corn dogs too and giving away free cookies with every combo meal.

As word spread about Milo's stand, cars were lined up for miles and miles, waiting to place their orders.

Mutzphey looked at Milo's stand and wondered, *what **is** his secret?*

He had a bright idea. He put on a costume and went over to spy out Milo's stand.

"Howdy, li'l pilgrim," said Mutzphey in his pretend cowboy voice.

"Ha, that's a funny disguise!" laughed Milo. "Why don't we do what's right in God's eyes and make up?"

"I'm not gonna do it! Now, move along.
This here town ain't big enough for the both of us!"
shouted Mutzphey.

"Uhh, I mean...you're copying
my ideas," he said as he
removed his disguise.

But he was still unwilling
to change.

Later that night, Mutzphey turned on his TV. "WHAT?" He was shocked.
Milo was being interviewed by the local news!
Mutzphey, feeling low, began to sing the blues.

Mutzphey turned up the volume. He heard his lifelong friend say, "...I want to thank God for His blessings, and I sure do miss my old friend, Mutzphey."

He could hardly believe his ears.

Touched in his heart by what he had just heard Milo say, Mutzphey sprang to his feet and looked up Milo's website.

He saw an ad that gave him hope:

"Milo's Lemonade: Help Wanted!"

"That's it!" shouted Mutzphey. "I'll find my favorite tie and ask him for a job!"

Early the next day, Mutzphey went and found Milo.

"Milo, I've come to applegize," said Mutzphey.

"You mean 'apologize,'" Milo laughed.

"Yeah, and this is my 'last stand.'"

Mutzphey fell to the ground, acting like he couldn't breathe, gasping for air. "Can I have a job?"

"Ah, Mutzphey, you don't have to carry on that way. The job is yours!"

And with that, they weren't just business partners, they were friends again. From that day on, Mutzphey and Milo would ***stand together!***